Hattie
&
Hudson

CHRIS VAN DUSEN

CANDLEWICK PRESS

Hattie McFadden loved to explore. Every morning after breakfast, she'd grab her life jacket, wave good-bye to her parents, and paddle out in the canoe to see what she could see.

Hattie discovered all kinds of things out on the lake.
She watched as a beaver tugged an alder branch slowly
through the water. Above, two bald eagles circled round
and round on wings broad and flat. And over in the cove,
a family of turtles with shiny black shells basked in the
warm summer sun.

Hattie was so happy, she started singing:

> *"When the sun is up and the day is new*
> *And the birds are a-singin' in the sky,*
> *That's when you'll find me in my little canoe,*
> *Paddle, just a-paddlin' by."*

She had no idea she was being heard.

Down at the bottom of the lake, in a cave dark and deep, there lived a mysterious creature. He was enormous but elusive. He never ventured up to the surface. He spent his days down below, all alone and out of sight.

The monster was used to hearing motors buzzing and propellers churning overhead. It was why he stayed hidden in his cave. But today he heard something different. A song, bouncy and bubbly, came echoing down through the water:

"So come with me 'cause there's room for two.
We'll be together, you and I,
Out on the lake in my little canoe,
Paddle, just a-paddlin' by."

It was so cheerful and charming that it drew the beast out of his lair and up toward the light.

He broke through the water, drawn by the music, and there, just off to his right, was a young girl, alone in a canoe, singing.

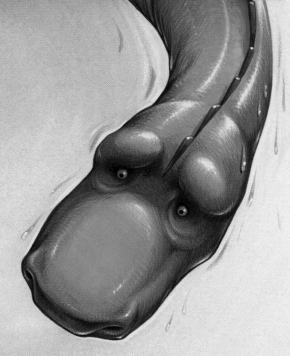

Hattie stopped when the thing rose right beside her. She stared at the monster and the monster stared back, but she didn't feel afraid. There was something in his eyes, the way he looked at her and the curious tilt of his head. It was almost as if he wanted to hear more. So Hattie softly continued singing:

"When the sun goes down and the day is through
And the moon is a-risin' in the sky,
I'll take you home in my little canoe,
Paddle, just a-paddlin' by."

And as she sang the last note, Hattie was astounded when the giant joined in, harmonizing with a low rumble.

Then someone screamed!

People pointed! Some fainted! Motors roared as boats fled in a frenzy!

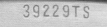

Amid all the commotion, the creature slid beneath the water,
and Hattie paddled slowly and silently back to the dock.

That night, Hattie tried to sleep, but every time she closed her eyes, she pictured the green, friendly face looking down at her. She wondered if she'd ever see him again. She decided she *had* to find out.

At the bottom of the lake, the girl's sweet song played over and over in the monster's head. He wondered if he'd ever see her again.
He decided *he* had to find out.

Hattie paddled the canoe quietly through the darkness. She stopped, waited, and looked down into the rippling water. Suddenly a massive black shape emerged from the depths. Two glowing eyes grew brighter and brighter as the shape drew closer and closer.

Slowly the gigantic head emerged from the water. It glistened in the moonlight. For a moment or two, the monster and the girl simply stared at each other.

Then Hattie broke the silence. "Hi. I'm Hattie," she said. "The girl you met this morning. I was really hoping I'd see you again. Uh . . . what's your name?"

The monster cocked his head.

"You do have a name, don't you?"

The monster raised his eyebrows and cocked his head even more.

"Hmmm. Maybe you don't," Hattie said. "Well, you kind of remind me of my uncle's dog, Hudson. Maybe I should call you Hudson. Do you like that name? Hudson?"

The monster slowly smiled.

"Good! I like it, too," she said. "It fits you. Hello, Hudson!"

And just like that, they became fast friends.

The little girl and the huge monster splashed and played in the silvery moonlight until Hattie realized it was time to head home.

As she climbed into the canoe, she turned around, smiling, and said, "Hey, Hudson. Let's meet again tomorrow night, okay?"

Hudson nodded eagerly and smiled back.

The next afternoon, there was a meeting at the
town hall. Everyone was yelling, suggesting ways
to get rid of what they called "the Deadly Beast."
If only they knew him, Hattie thought.

She tried to say something, but she was interrupted.
She tried again, but no one heard her.
She tried several times to speak.
Finally she gave up.

When the meeting was over, Hattie walked home
with her dad. She felt a little sick.

Hattie snuck out again that night to be with Hudson,
but when they met, she didn't feel much like playing.

"The townspeople saw you yesterday," she explained.
"Everybody thinks you're dangerous. Tomorrow they're
coming to catch you and take you away. I don't know
where to, but we can't let this happen. We need a plan."

Hattie was deep in thought when Hudson abruptly nudged
the canoe with his nose, nearly knocking it over.

"Hey!" barked Hattie.

Hudson did it again.

"What the heck?"

Once again, he bumped the boat. Then he looked at her
and smiled brightly.

"Wait a second. I think I know what you're doing,"
said Hattie. Then she added, "And this could work.
This could definitely work!
Hudson, you're a genius!"

At the break of dawn, Hattie paddled her canoe over
to the town landing. The men were already gathered,
loading their boats with radars, ropes, and netting.
Hattie started to feel sick again.

But she had to stay focused.
She had to stick to the plan.
She had to save her new friend.

So she paddled her canoe away from the shore
and to the center of the lake. Then she waited.

Now it was Hudson's turn.
He swam up to Hattie.
He carefully bumped the bottom of the canoe.
It flipped over easily, tossing Hattie, as planned,
into the water.

Hattie flailed her arms!
She splashed the water!
She pretended to be in serious peril!
The men on the landing sprang into action.
"Hang on!" someone hollered. "We're on our way!"

The boats were coming quickly, but Hattie waited
and waited until they were in perfect position.
Then she signaled to Hudson.

The people stared in complete, stunned silence as Hudson slowly swam past. When he reached the landing, he gently lowered his head so Hattie could slide off.

Now it was Hattie's turn to hold a meeting.

"This is Hudson," she said bravely. "He's a friend of mine. I know you think he's scary and mean and dangerous, but he's actually very friendly. He won't hurt you, I promise. This lake is his home, and I think he deserves to stay. Once you get to know him, I'm sure you'll agree."

Hattie paused.

Everyone stood still.

Then a young boy slowly walked up and patted Hudson gently on the nose. Another child followed. Then another.

Soon, a few adults cautiously stepped forward.

Before long, a crowd had gathered around Hudson.

It took some convincing, but eventually everyone welcomed the idea of having Hudson around. He even became something of an attraction. People traveled from far and wide to spend time with the famous friendly monster.

But when the sun went down and the visitors left, for Hattie and Hudson, everything was just as it had been since the beginning. And every night they met in the same place, played the same games, and splashed and frolicked under the big silver summer moon.

My idea of a perfect day is to be on a lake, in Maine,
with Lori, Ethan, and Tucker, to whom this book is lovingly dedicated.

A monster-size thank-you to Savannah for being my "Hattie." Thanks also to Tommy and Hillary for letting me use their perfect camp as a model; to the Ford family for naming rights; to my editor, Joan Powers, for carefully tweaking nine different versions of this story (I counted!); and to my art director, Ann Stott, for her endless patience and expert eye.

And to all the young explorers who will be spending time at a lake this summer: Remember, there are no such things as lake monsters. They don't exist. At least I've never seen one. But I keep looking.

First paperback edition 2021

Library of Congress Catalog Card Number 2015933241
ISBN 978-0-7636-6545-6 (hardcover)
ISBN 978-1-5362-1738-4 (paperback)

21 22 23 24 25 26 CCP 10 9 8 7 6 5 4 3 2 1

Printed in Shenzhen, Guangdong, China

This book was typeset in Cushing.
The illustrations were done in gouache.

Candlewick Press
99 Dover Street
Somerville, Massachusetts 02144

www.candlewick.com